KV-638-960

There is no one method or technique that is the ONLY way to learn to read. Children learn in a variety of ways. **Read with me** is an enjoyable and uncomplicated scheme that will give your child reading confidence. Through exciting stories about Kate, Tom and Sam the dog, **Read with me**:

- *teaches the first 300 key words (75% of our everyday language) plus 500 additional words*

- *stimulates a child's language and imagination through humorous, full colour illustration*

- *introduces situations and events children can relate to*

- *encourages and develops conversation and observational skills*

- *support material includes Practice and Play Books, Flash Cards, Book and Cassette Packs*

Always praise and encourage as you go along. Keep your reading sessions short and stop immediately if your child loses interest.

Ladybird books are widely available, but in case of
difficulty may be ordered by post or telephone from:

Ladybird Books – Cash Sales Department
Littlegate Road  Paignton  Devon TQ3 3BE
Telephone 0803 554761

A catalogue record for this book is available
from the British Library

Published by Ladybird Books Ltd  Loughborough  Leicestershire  UK
Ladybird Books Inc  Auburn  Maine 04210  USA

Printed in EC

# Read with me
# A busy night

by WILLIAM MURRAY
stories by JILL CORBY
illustrated by TERRY BURTON

Tom and Kate were sitting at the table eating. Their mother was busy getting their lunch boxes ready, so they were talking to their father.

"You are slow today, Tom and Kate," said their mother. "You will have to stop talking and eat up your apples and drink your milk."

"Yes," said Dad. "Eat up that apple quickly, Kate. And Tom, you still have some milk left. You two are very slow today." Mother took two red apples. She put one apple in Kate's lunch box, and the other in Tom's lunch box.

"I have also put some jam cakes in your boxes today," Mum told them. "And your milk drinks are ready here."

"I like jam cakes," said Tom. "Lots of jam cakes."

"Don't forget that you are going swimming with John and his dad after school today," Dad told them as he gave Tom some money.

"Your swimming things are in the bags by the door," Mum said.

"Come on," she said. "I'm ready to go. You two are very slow today. It will be the afternoon by the time you get to school." So Tom and Kate got all their things and said goodbye to their dad.

As they were walking to school, Tom asked his mum what she was going to do while they were at school. She told him that she had to clean the house first, and then go to the shops.

"Can you get some apples and jam?" asked Kate.

"Yes, and this afternoon, little Lucy and her mum are coming round. We are going to make lots of things for the school," she said. "It's a good thing that I haven't got to go to work today."

When Mum got back home she started to clean the house.

"This house needs a good clean," she told Sam. "It will keep me busy all morning. And I must be back from the shops before Lucy and her mother come this afternoon."

"Go and have a sleep now, Sam, and I'll start cleaning," she said. "I must have everything done by this afternoon."

So she went into Tom's room and started to tidy and clean it. She made the bed and looked at Tom's gerbils playing.

"Gerbils need to sleep in the day time. Go to sleep, gerbils," she told them.

Then she went into Kate's room and started to clean and tidy it. She made the bed and she looked at Kate's dolls' house.

"Kate has worked hard," she said to herself. "She has made the dolls' house nice and tidy."

Then she saw a big bee in the room.

"I must open the window so that the bee can fly out," she told herself.

She left the window open so that the bee could fly out. Then she went on cleaning the house.

When she had the house clean and sparkling, she went to look for the bee. She couldn't see it anywhere.

"I must shut that window," she told herself.
(BUT YOU CAN SEE THAT BEE CAN'T YOU?)

Then she went to get ready to go to the shops. She put on her jacket and shut all the windows. She also shut the door.

Then Sam saw a big brown dog and wanted to say hello. But Mum would not let him.

"Come on, Sam," she told him. "You can't be slow today."

Mum left Sam outside the shop, in the sun, and went in to buy some eggs, jam and apples and other things.

When Mum came out of the shop, she saw that the sun had gone in and it was cold and windy. So she took Sam home quickly.

"It's so cold now that I think I'll put the fire on," she said to herself. "The fire will warm the place up."

She took out all the things that they would need to make the animals for the school sale and put them on the table. The school often had a sale, but this sale would be a very big one. Many mothers and fathers were making things for it.

Then Sam started to bark, and she knew that little Lucy and her mother had already come. She went to let them in.

"Now that the sun has gone in, it's getting very cold outside," Lucy's mother said. "But it's lovely and warm in here with the fire on."

"I'll put all these toys down on the carpet by the fire for Lucy," said Mum. "Then she will be quite warm. And here is some milk for her."

They sat down to start making the toy animals for the sale. Lucy sat down on the carpet with all the toys around her. But she cried and cried.

"What's the matter, Lucy?" her mother asked. "Don't cry. Please don't cry."

"Don't want toys. Don't want milk," Lucy shouted.

Then she did a very naughty thing. She kicked the toys and she kicked her milk. She kicked so hard that the toys went everywhere and the milk went all over the carpet.

"Lucy, stop that," her mother said. "That was a very naughty thing to do, very naughty. Just look at the carpet."

And she picked her up and talked to her quietly. But Lucy cried and cried and kicked and kicked. She didn't want to be picked up, and she didn't want her mum to talk.

"Would you like a sleep, Lucy?" her mother asked.

But Lucy just cried and cried.

"She will feel better when she has had a sleep," her mother said.

So she took Lucy and quietly put her in Kate's bed for a sleep. Then she went back to make the animals for the sale.

Then the bee started to buzz around Lucy's head. It went buzz, buzz all around her head and all around the room. As she looked at it, she saw that it was going to buzz around her head once more.

"Bad bee. Bad bee," she said as she got out of bed.

Then the bee went into Kate's dolls' house.

The bee went buzzing round all the rooms in Kate's dolls' house. Lucy tried very hard to get it out. She tried so hard that lots of things fell over. She tried and tried to get the bee out and more things fell over. Some fell on the carpet. Now there was an awful mess in Kate's room.

Then it came buzzing around Lucy's head again.

"Bad bee, very bad bee," she shouted at it. "Fly away."

The bee did fly away. It flew away from the awful mess and into Tom's room. Lucy saw it go and she went too, to see where the bee went. She saw it buzzing round and round, then it went on the gerbils' cage.

Lucy didn't like the bee on the cage, and she could see that the gerbils had all gone to sleep. So she tried to get the bee off. She bumped the cage so hard that it fell over. The door came open letting the gerbils run out of the cage and away from the awful mess. They ran under Tom's bed.

Now Lucy knew that she had done a very naughty thing letting the gerbils out of their cage.

She looked under Tom's bed to see if she could find them. But they had all gone. Then she saw the bee again. It went buzzing around her head once more and then flew out of the window.

"Bad bee gone," she told herself. Then she went back into Kate's room and got into bed and went quietly to sleep.

The two mothers were having a very busy time at the table making animals for the sale. They didn't know that Lucy had made an awful mess upstairs.

"Lucy has been asleep a long time today," her mother said. "I shall have to go upstairs and bring her down now."

So Lucy's mother went upstairs to get her. She saw that Lucy was asleep, but she didn't see the awful mess around Kate's dolls' house. She didn't see that Tom's gerbils had gone. But she did see that Lucy had come out in spots, all over her face.

"She is not well. That's why she was so naughty," she said to herself quietly, and picked Lucy up.

"Oh dear, I'm very sorry that Lucy has spots," Mum said. "But she will be better soon."

At the end of school, Kate and Tom got all their things and went with John to meet his dad, Mr Hunt.

''Now we can all go swimming,'' he told them.

The sun had already gone in and it was quite cold.

They didn't have long to wait for the bus and Mr Hunt paid for their tickets. They got off the bus by the swimming pool.

Tom took out his money.

''You paid for the bus ride, Mr Hunt, so please may I buy the tickets for us to swim?'' Tom asked.

"Thank you very much, Tom,"
Mr Hunt said. "That would be very
nice."

So Tom paid for them all to go in and
the girl gave him some change. Tom
put the change in his bag.

"I'll change in here," Kate told them.
"You will have to go upstairs to
change. So I'll see you soon by the
pool."

They were all having
a good time and
Kate went down the
water slide for the
very first time.

When they were ready, Mr Hunt said, ''We must see if the café is open or closed.''

''The café is often closed at this time of day,'' John told them.

''You may be right, John, the café may be closed, but we will just go and see,'' Mr Hunt said.

So they all went upstairs to the café. There was a sign on the door that said 'CLOSED'. A girl inside was just coming to turn the sign round and change it from 'CLOSED' to 'OPEN'.

So they all went into the café.

''What would you like to eat?'' Mr Hunt asked them. ''You will need something to eat after all that swimming.''

John said that he would like sausages, eggs, chips and beans with a drink of orange. Then Mr Hunt asked Kate and Tom if they would also like sausages, eggs, chips and beans.

"I love sausages," said Kate. "Yes, please."

"And I love eggs, chips and beans as well," said Tom. "Yes, please."

"I love it all," John told them.

So Mr Hunt paid for them all to have sausages, eggs, chips and beans.

They all went home on the bus. Kate looked out of the window. "Why does that bus have P-R-I-V-A-T-E on it?" she asked.

"That bus is going to take a lot of people from one place to another place. It won't stop for people like us to get on it."

"And there was a door at the swimming pool that had PRIVATE on it," Tom said.

"Well," said Mr Hunt, "the PRIVATE sign on the door is there so that only people who work there go in. People like us must not go in. There may be danger in that place."

"So we can never go in when we see the PRIVATE sign?" asked Tom.

"That's quite right," Mr Hunt told them. "This is our stop. We must get off here and go home, or your mum and dad will think we have got lost."

When they got to their door, Mum was already there.

"We were just saying that you must have got lost," she told them.

"But we're very pleased that you're not lost," Dad said. "Come in out of the cold and get warm by the fire."

Tom and Kate told their dad and mum
all about swimming and how they had
had sausages, eggs, chips and beans
to eat. Dad had already made them
all a hot milk drink to warm them up.

Then Mr Hunt said that it was time
that he took John home.

"Thank you for the drink," he said.
"We must go home now, or Mrs Hunt
will think that we are lost."

Tom and Kate said thank you for taking them to the swimming pool.

"Do you know," said Kate, "I've been going swimming for a year and I've only just started to swim well in the deep end. Tom's been swimming in the deep end for a long time, but I couldn't go down the water slide into the deep end for a year."

Then Dad said that she had done very well to be swimming in the deep end after only a year.

"But a year is a very long time," Kate told him.

"It may be a long time when you're little," Dad said. "But as you get bigger, the years go by faster and faster."

"So for Granny the years go by very quickly?" asked Tom.

"They go by too quickly when you are as old as I am," laughed Dad. "And now it's time for bed."

Tom and Kate went upstairs. Kate found an awful mess in her room, and Tom also saw an awful mess in his room. They shouted to their dad and mum to come and look.

Kate cried, "Just look at my dolls' house. Everything is broken. There is nothing left. It's all broken up."

And Tom cried, "My gerbils have gone. The cage is open. Where can my gerbils have gone?"

Mum and Dad came running upstairs to see what was the matter. They looked at the awful mess and all the broken things.

"Who could have made this mess?" asked Dad.

"I know who it was," said Mum. "It was Lucy."

She told them how naughty Lucy had been and that she went to sleep in Kate's bed. And how she had spots all over her face.

"I love my dolls' house, and look at it now," cried Kate. "That's the end of my dolls' house. There is nothing left."

"And I love my gerbils, and now they have all gone," cried Tom. "That's the last of my gerbils. There is nothing left of them."

Mum and Dad could see that they were very, very sad.

"We will mend everything tomorrow, Kate. And Tom, we will put something in the cage for the gerbils to eat," Dad told them.

They left the cage door open so that the gerbils could get in.

"We will mend everything tomorrow," Mum said. "Everything will be better tomorrow, you'll see."

Tom and Kate were very sad. They got into bed. Kate looked at all the broken things and said to herself, "I love all my little things and Dad can't mend all of them. That's the end of them. There is nothing left but lots of bits."

Tom looked at his broken cage and said to himself, "I love my gerbils but they will never come back now. That's the last of them. They are all lost."

After a long time, they went to sleep.

The first thing Tom saw was that his gerbils were back. They were running around all over the place. He got out of bed to catch them and put them back in the cage. But they ran everywhere so quickly that he couldn't catch any of them. He went to get Kate to help him to catch the gerbils.

"Get up, Kate, get up. The gerbils are back. Please will you help me catch them?" he asked.

The gerbils were in Kate's room now, and they were looking at the awful mess.

"Just look at that dolls' house," said one gerbil to the others. "What a mess. Fancy letting it get into a mess like that."

Tom and Kate were very surprised to hear the gerbils talking.

"It wasn't me. I didn't let it get into a mess like that," Kate told them. "It was naughty Lucy who did it. But she wasn't very well."

"Can we mend it and make it tidy again?" asked the little gerbil.

"Can you really fix it for me?" asked Kate, in surprise.

"We can mend anything," the big gerbil told them. "I'll get my tools," he said. "Then we can fix everything."

And he went under Kate's bed. In a minute or two he came back with his tools.

"Hold this, Tom," he said. "And you hold these, Kate."

"This won't work," Tom told Kate.
"We are too big to use these tools."

"We can fix that for you, too," the
other gerbil said. "You just have to go
round and round backwards as fast
as you can and say rellams lots of
times."

"Why rellams?" asked Tom.

"Silly, silly, silly," said the little gerbil,
jumping up and down. "Rellams is
smaller backwards. If you want to get
smaller, you have to say rellams."

So Kate went round and round backwards, faster and faster.

"Rellams, rellams, rellams," she said, as she went smaller and smaller. Soon she was much smaller, the same size as the gerbils. But Tom wasn't, he looked enormous. He was so enormous that he was really quite scary.

"Come on, Tom," she told him. "It's your turn now."

So Tom also went round and round backwards saying rellams, rellams, rellams.

Then he was smaller too, the same size as Kate and the gerbils.

"That's much better," said the big gerbil. "You're smaller now. We're all the same size and we can all use the tools. We will fix everything much more quickly. Bring me the red chair first, please. Then you can bring me the smaller chair."

So they all started work. The little gerbil picked up the chairs, one by one, and took them out to the big gerbil. The other gerbil started to clean the dolls' house.

"Bring me the table now, please," said the big gerbil.

Tom and Kate took out the table and the other things and then they started to mend them.

They were very busy for a long time. But in the end it was all done.

"That's lovely," Kate told them. "It looks just as nice now as it did before. Thank you all very much."

Then the gerbils asked Kate and Tom if they would like to come and see where they lived.

"But you live in the cage in my room," Tom told them.

"We only live there in the day," the big gerbil said. "At night we live in our own home."

"But you can't get out of the cage," said Tom. "I always make sure I keep it shut at night."

"We know that you keep the door shut," said the other gerbil. "We always use a little hole that we made at the back."

Then they told Tom and Kate how they came out of their cage every night and went to their real home.

"But the cage is your real home," said Tom. "You have something to eat, some water to drink, and a nice warm bed. You don't need anything more."

"Yes, we do," the gerbils all said at once.

"What do you need then?" asked Tom.

"Chairs to sit on and a table to eat off," the big gerbil said.

"And carpets to walk on," the other gerbil said.

"And a fire to keep us warm when it's cold," the little gerbil said.

"We need a real home," the big gerbil said.

"Now that you are the same size as us, would you like to come and see our real home?" asked the big gerbil.

"Yes, please," said Kate and Tom.

"Bring them through the hole," he told the other two.

So they all had to squeeze through the hole under Kate's bed. And it really was a squeeze to get through.

"It is quite a squeeze," the big gerbil said. "But if we had made the hole any bigger, your mother could have seen it when she was cleaning."

When they were all through, they shut the door. Then they sat down on the chairs. Kate sat by the fire with the little gerbil.

"Tell me," asked Tom, "why don't you have any names?"

"That's your fault," said the big gerbil.

"Yes, it's not our fault," said the next gerbil.

"It's all your fault," said the little gerbil.

Tom looked surprised and sad.

"How can it be my fault?" he asked.

"Because you never gave us any names, so it's all your fault," the little gerbil told him.

"Oh dear," said Tom. "I'm very sorry. I'm very sorry that I didn't give you any names."

"Yes," said Kate. "We really are sorry. You must all have a name. What would you like your names to be?"

"I'll be George," said the big gerbil.

"I'll be Gemma," said the next gerbil.

"And I'll be Grace," said the little gerbil.

"George, Gemma and Grace," said Kate. "That's lovely."

"Why didn't you use those names before," asked Tom, "if you know that you like them?"

But George, Gemma and Grace were all having a drink and they didn't hear Tom.

Then George told them that they would all have to go as it would soon be day. They had to get back into their cage and Tom and Kate had to get back into bed.

"We'll have to squeeze through that hole again," Tom told Kate.

So they all went through the hole.
Kate looked at her bed. It looked
enormous.

"I can't get up there," she told
George, Gemma and Grace.
"It's much too high. It's enormous."

"Silly, silly, silly," said Grace.
"Turn the other way round."

"And say reggib, reggib, reggib," said
Gemma.

Kate and Tom said, "Reggib, reggib,
reggib," and got bigger and bigger as
they went round and round. They
thanked the gerbils for letting them
see their other home. Then they went
back to bed and fell asleep.

The next morning, Dad came to tell Tom to get up.

"Look, Dad," Tom said. "George, Gemma and Grace are all back. They are all asleep."

So Dad, looking surprised, shut the cage door and went to tell Kate to get up.

"Look, Dad," Kate said. "Look at my dolls' house. It's all tidy. George, Gemma and Grace made it tidy."

This time Dad was so surprised that he told Mum to come and look.

"There is nothing left to do," he told her. "Everything is mended."

Then Tom and Kate told them how they mended the chairs first with George's tools. And then how they had mended all the other things.

"But you can't use tools," Dad said.

"We can use tools now," Tom told him. "George told us how to use them and we all mended everything."

"You must have had a very exciting time, with all that going on in the night," Dad said.

"Yes," said Tom. "And now we have to fix signs on our doors."

"What will you put on the signs?" asked Dad.

"PRIVATE," said Tom and Kate at the same time.

"Then Lucy can't come in," Kate told them.

Mum laughed and said, "You had better make sure that she can read."

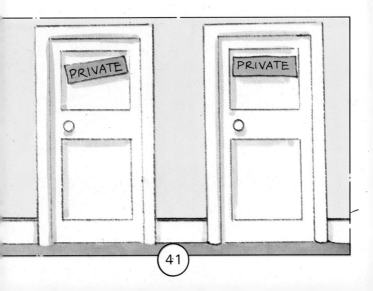

## Words introduced in this book

Number of words.....................................82

\* These are made-up words necessary for the story.

*Talk about the picture.*
*Can you remember what Tom's gerbils were called?*

*Where did they live?*

*What would you like to have as a pet?*

# LADYBIRD
# READING SCHEMES

Ladybird reading schemes are suitable for use
with any other method of learning to read.

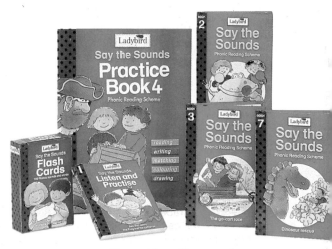

## Say the Sounds

Ladybird's **Say the Sounds** graded reading scheme is a
*phonics* scheme. It teaches children the sounds of individual
letters and letter combinations, enabling them to tackle new
words by building them up as a blend of smaller units.

*There are 8 titles in this scheme:*

1 **Rocket to the jungle**
2 **Frog and the lollipops**
3 **The go-cart race**
4 **Pirate's treasure**
5 **Humpty Dumpty and the robots**
6 **Flying saucer**
7 **Dinosaur rescue**
8 **The accident**

*Support material available:* Practice Books, Double Cassette Pack,
Flash Cards